Rainbow Fish & Friends

HIDDEN TREASURES

TEXT BY GAIL DONOVAN

ILLUSTRATIONS BY DAVID AUSTIN CLAR STUDIO

Night Sky Books
New York • London

"Don't forget," said Miss Cuttle, "tomorrow is show-and-tell. I want each of you to bring in something that you treasure."

"Treasure?" worried Rusty. "You mean like gold coins?"

"Not necessarily," explained Miss Cuttle. "A treasure can be anything—anything at all. It just has to mean something special to you."

"I already know what I'm going to share!" shouted Rainbow Fish.

The next morning the school cave bubbled with excitement. Then, just as they were about to begin, a loud noise rumbled outside.

"I'll be right back," said Miss Cuttle as she rushed out to investigate. "I expect all of you to behave while I'm away."

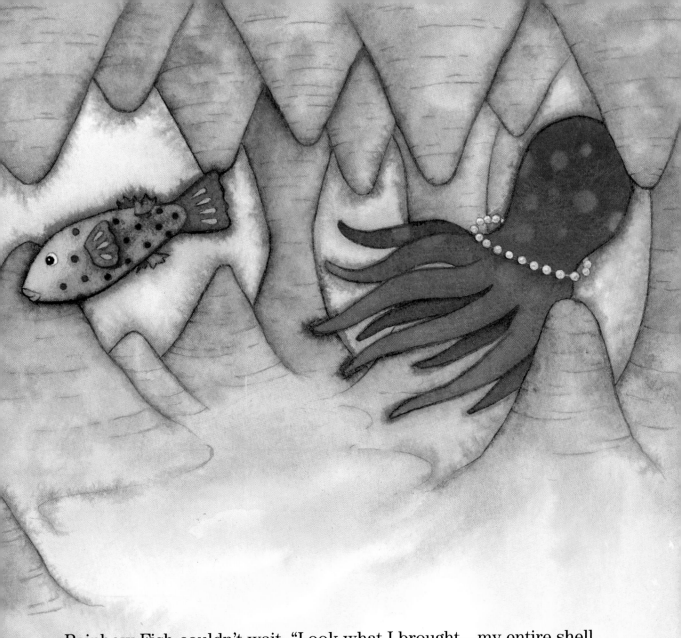

Rainbow Fish couldn't wait. "Look what I brought—my entire shell collection! Each one is special and reminds me of a different friend."

"But that's a million things," objected Puffer, "not one special thing. Now my pebble is extra extraordinary! Look how smooth it is! It probably crashed in the waves for a billion years!"

"Oh, Puffer, there you go exaggerating again!" cried Angel as she unfurled her map. "This has been in my family for ages. My great-grandfather discovered it in the captain's room of a sunken ship. Every place I've ever called home is on this map."

"My compass came from an old ship, too," said Rusty. "Whenever I worry that I'm lost, it always shows me the way home. My trusty compass hasn't failed me yet."

"Isn't your trusty compass a bit rusty, old Rusty?" asked Rosie. "Now *my* treasure is nice and shiny."

"I used to play with this when I was little. When Pearl was born, the very first thing I said was, she's as pretty as my pink pearl. So we named her Pearl!"

Then Pearl showed the class her seaweed doll. "Rosie made her for me and I sleep with her every night."

"I brought something that I always sleep with, too," said Tug. "It keeps away all my bad dreams."

"It's a real shark's tooth," said Tug. "Remember when Rainbow Fish rescued me from the shark?"

"But this tooth isn't from that shark, is it?" asked Little Blue. "You just found some old shark's fallen-out tooth, right? So that shouldn't count."

"Anyway, sharks lose teeth all the time," added Puffer. "They have zillions of teeth so that's not so special!"

"It doesn't have to be from that same shark to be special!" explained Dyna.

"Thanks, Dyna," said Tug, "what did you bring?"

"I brought in an algae I grew myself. It glows just like my lightning streak. It's phosphorescent."

"You mean *slimy*," said Spike. "Check out my treasure. It's my lucky sand dollar."

"I saw you find that on your way to school! How special could that be?" asked Rainbow Fish. "What about you, Little Blue? You're the last one. What did you bring?"

"My scale," announced Little Blue. "The one you gave me, Rainbow Fish."

Rainbow Fish smiled.

"Should that count?" asked Spike.

"That's like bringing in your *fin* for sharing," added Rosie.

Everyone began arguing about what could count and what couldn't.

"Quiet!" interrupted Rusty. "Do you want to get us into trouble?"

"I don't think we're supposed to be fighting about what counts as special to somebody else!" added Tug.

Rainbow Fish agreed. "That's right, I felt really bad when no one liked my shells."

"Me, too!" echoed one fish after another. "Me, too!"

"I think we should start again," Dyna suggested. "Truce?"

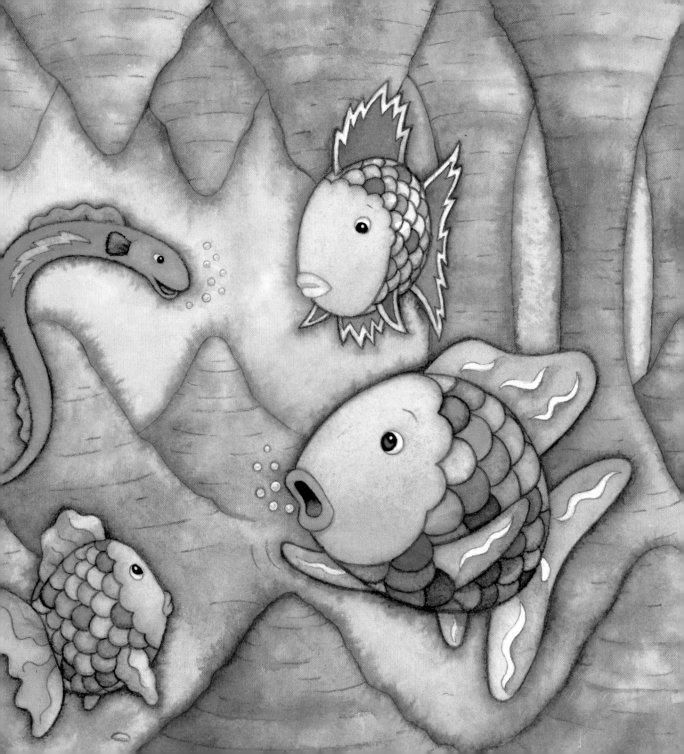

Just as they agreed to the truce, Miss Cuttle jetted back into the cave, apologizing for her absence. "The noise was nothing but a large ship passing on the water's surface. Now, let's get started," she said, "and remember, just as each of you is special, so are the things you brought."

"We know!" They laughed.

"What's so funny?" asked Miss Cuttle.

"Oh, nothing," said Rainbow Fish, smiling at the others as they began to spread out their treasures.

Night Sky Books
A division of North-South Books Inc.

Copyright © 2001 by Nord-Süd Verlag, AG, Gossau Zürich, Switzerland
First published in Switzerland under the title *Der grösste Schatz*
English translation copyright © 2001 by NIGHT SKY BOOKS, a
division of North-South Books, Inc., New York

First published in the United States, Great Britain,
Canada, Australia, and New Zealand in 2001 by
NIGHT SKY BOOKS, a division of North-South Books Inc.

ISBN 1-59014-003-6
1 3 5 7 9 10 8 6 4 2
Printed in Belgium

For more information about our books, and the authors and artists
who create them, visit our website: www.northsouth.com